HALLOWEEN,
HERE I COME!

For Cousin Jon Braver, the King of Halloween—DJS

For Nick, Harrison, Olivia, and Jaxon—LS

GROSSET & DUNLAP
An Imprint of Penguin Random House LLC, New York

Text copyright © 2020 by David Steinberg. Illustrations copyright © 2020 by Laurie Stansfield.
All rights reserved. Published by Grosset & Dunlap, an imprint of Penguin Random House LLC, New York.
GROSSET & DUNLAP is a registered trademark of Penguin Random House LLC.
Manufactured in China.

Visit us online at www.penguinrandomhouse.com.

Library of Congress Control Number: 2019054769

ISBN 9780593094204   10 9 8 7 6 5 4 3 2 1

HALLOWEEN, HERE I COME!

BY D. J. STEINBERG

ILLUSTRATED BY LAURIE STANSFIELD

GROSSET & DUNLAP

DO NOT READ THIS BOOK!

This book is too scary!
Don't read it—look out!
There are gonna be **goblins** and **zombies**,
no doubt!

4

You may meet a **ghost** . . .
maybe **vampire bats**!
There are sure to be **witches**
with creepy **black cats**!
Last chance! Close the book!
Scary things lie ahead . . .

You're still here?!
Did you hear *one word* I said?!
See, just like I warned you—the gang is all here . . .
and they're waiting for you with some Halloween cheer!

THE PERFECT PUMPKIN

It's hard to pick a pumpkin,
but we found the *perfect* one.

Now Daddy has to lug it home,
because it weighs a ton!

A BUNCH OF GRAPES

Teddy is a bunch of grapes,
with balloons from bottom to top.
He stays on his feet all Halloween long,
'cause if he sits down . . . he'll go—*POP!*

WHICH WITCH HAS A COLD?

Annie's got a twitch in her nose,
now a sneeze,
next a wheeze,
then a crackle!
"Oh, bats!" Annie says to her cat and her broom—
"I'm a witch, but I've lost my cackle!"

THE PUMPKIN PATCH

Down the road is an empty lot
where my friends and I play catch,
but once a year it magically
becomes the pumpkin patch.

Presto! It suddenly appears
one crisp October day—
a spooky fence, a pumpkin tent,
a maze made out of hay.

All the families come round
just as they have for years,
till—*presto!*—midnight on Halloween,
that pumpkin patch d i s a p p e a r s.

CLOSING
MIDNIGHT
OCTOBER 31st

TWENTY THOUSAND JACKS

I love my jack-o'-lantern,
but why is it named *Jack*?
It looks more like a Ziggy or a Boris or a Shaq.
Over there—that one's a Phoebe.
And that one looks like a Bing . . .
So why are all these pumpkins
called *exactly* the same thing?

MY SKELETON GUY

My class made skeletons today.
Come meet my *skele*-guy!
I made him wear a *skele*-hat
and a fancy *skele*-tie.
I gave him a snappy *skele*-vest
and some schnazzy *skele*-pants,
and then—*look*—I made my *skele*-dude
dance a happy *skele*-dance!

COSTUME POP-UP SHOP

I think I'll be a bumblebee.
A bumblebee, that's what I'll be . . .
But when I slip into the shop,
I think my eyes are gonna pop!

A billion costumes fill the aisles:
hats and wigs and masks for miles,
poofy gowns and sparkly crowns,
hairy werewolves, scary clowns,
lions, tigers, kangaroos . . .
How's a kid supposed to choose?!

"Can I help?" asks the cashier.
"Yes, I'd like one of **everything** here."
She *seems* to find this kind of funny
and asks if I have *that* much money.
Hmmm, I know how much I brought with me . . .
Looks like I'll be a bumblebee!

TRICK OR TREAT

Trick or treat,
trick or treat,
everybody to the street!
Ring the bells,
keep buckets handy—
let's all go and get some candy!

19

A MUMMY NAMED MAY

There once was a mummy named May
who worried she might lose her way,
but wherever she traveled,
her wrapping unraveled,
which led her back home every day!

THE UNICORN'S HORN

A pink unicorn known as Toni
took a path that was scraggly and stony.
When her hood snagged a tree,
her horn twisted free,
which is how she became a pink *pony*.

HALLOWEEN JITTERS

My little brother wouldn't go.
At the door, he screamed,
"NO, NO!"

I took his hand and led the way.
"I promise, it'll be okay . . ."
I showed how trick-or-treating's done.
The two of us had so much fun . . .

that when we got back to our door,
my little brother screamed,
"MORE, MORE!"

A TON OF TREATS

My feet are tired of walking,
and my mouth is tired of talking,
and my arms are tired of carrying this sack.
It didn't weigh a thing at first,
but—*wow!*—now it's about to burst
with all the treats I'll eat when I get back!

THE HOUSE AT THE END OF THE STREET

Scary music fills the air.
A wooden sign warns *BEWARE!*
Something rustles in the night—
glowing yellow eyes shine bright.

In the moonlight, gravestones gleam—
skeletons pop up and scream.
Up the stairs, we hear heartbeats . . .
A bony arm hands us some treats.

BEWARE

Take that candy, grab on tight,
and *run-run-run* with all your might!

27

Now we hold our breath and count to ten . . .
and then sneak back in line again!

SORTING THE LOOT

All the treats that are healthy,
I'll give to my mother.
All the ones that are melty
will go to my brother.
All the good ones I'm keeping,
because they're too yummy.
And the best ones of all . . .
well, they're now in my tummy!

DOUBLE LUCK!

Hey, look! Double luck!
My tooth got stuck
while chomping a jelly bean.
It jiggled right out,
which made me shout:

"The Tooth Fairy's coming on Halloween!"

(Think she'll be wearing a costume? How funny . . .
if the Tooth Fairy comes as the Easter Bunny!)

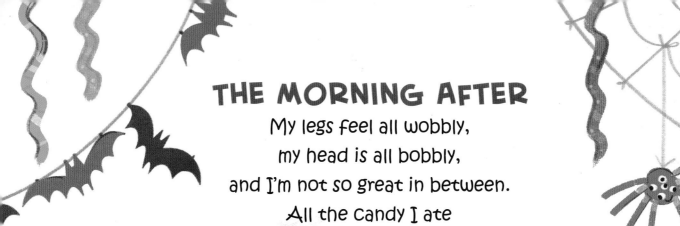

THE MORNING AFTER

My legs feel all wobbly,
my head is all bobbly,
and I'm not so great in between.
All the candy I ate
left me in this sad state—
but I'll be better by *next* Halloween!